Sometimes YOU find a RED Rhinoceros

by Andy Myer

The opinions expressed by the Author are not necessarily those held by PYP Academy Press.

Ordering Information: Quantity sales and special discounts are available on quantity purchases by corporations, associations, and others. For details, contact the author at author email address.

Printed in the United States of America.
ISBN: 978-1-951591-92-2 (hardcover)
ISBN: 978-1-951591-93-9 (paperback)

Library of Congress Control Number 2021913542

ACADEMY
PRESS

Sometimes YOU find a RED Rhinoceros

by Andy Myer

PYP
ACADEMY
PRESS

Sometimes you find a red rhinoceros.

You feed it some dandelions, which happen to be its favorite food in the whole world.

Sometimes it lets you
climb up on its back to
show Mom and Dad
who holler...

And you do!!
Every week
you wash your
red rhinoceros
in the driveway
with soap and
water,

and powder its butt, so it won't smell quite so rhinoceros-y.

Sometimes you take your rhinoceros out for long walks, to munch on grass and flowers,

even though neighbors run over to yell at you for ruining their nice yards.

so everyone has to leave the building,

and the fire department comes.

Then the animal control guy comes to your house.
He says, "You can't have a rhinoceros as a pet."

So you have to hide your red rhinoceros.

Then one day, you have to sit down with your red rhinoceros and say, "I'm sorry, this isn't really working out that well."

And you and your rhinoceros have a good cry.

So you pack up your red rhinoceros's things, and slowly walk to the zoo,...

...and you find a kind zookeeper

"Could you take my red rhinoceros?" you ask.

"It will do ANYTHING for dandelions, and would love to play with other rhinoceroses." "I know just the spot," replies the zookeeper.

You turn to your red rhinoceros and say, "Goodbye! I promise I'll visit soon!"

And you do! On sunny days you go to the zoo and visit your red rhinoceros.

You wave and shout, "HI! IT'S ME!"

You finally wave goodbye...

...and run all the way home feeling
VERY happy!!

Over his wide-ranging career, Andy Myer has been a freelance humorous illustrator, writer, graphic designer, and corporate communications consultant. His first published book, *The Liberated Father's Handbook*, was released by St. Martin's Press in 1983. In the decades that followed his witty words and images have appeared in national consumer and trade publications, the commentary pages of major newspapers, and in diverse graphic and editorial assignments in advertising, publishing, and business.

Andy made his first appearance as a children's book author/illustrator with *Pickles, Please!*, published by Running Press Kids in 2011. His second picture book, *Delia's Dull Day*, was released by Sleeping Bear Press in 2012.

Andy's next book, *Henry Hubble's Book of Troubles* (Delacorte Press, 2015), was his first project for middle grade readers.

He lives in Ambler, Pennsylvania with his wife Sandi, happily surrounded by his children and grandchildren.

If you loved the book, or have questions for Andy, you can reach him at info@redrhinocerosbook.com.

Call to Action!

The rhinoceros is an amazing animal, but there aren't many left in the world because they're hunted for their horns, and the places where they live are quickly disappearing. Would you like to help keep rhinos safe? You can!! There's a group that works hard to protect them, and many other endangered animals— it's the World Wildlife Fund at www.worldwildlife.org/. It would be wonderful if you could raise money, build support for the animals online, or share your concern with your classmates and friends!

Can you think of another animal (or elf, or genie, or unusual being) that would be strange to "find?" What if you took it home with you? Can you make your own story about what might happen?

There are other activities and questions about this book at www.redrhinocerosbook.com. Check it out!!

Photo by Jean Van Der Meulen/Pixbay

CPSIA information can be obtained
at www.ICGtesting.com
Printed in the USA
BVHW091258181121
621928BV00009B/435

* 9 7 8 1 9 5 1 5 9 1 9 2 2 *